Shatterproof

Jocelyn Shipley

Orca currents

ORCA BOOK PUBLISHERS

For Seth, Eva, James, Lucas,
Lauren and Iris

Library and Archives Canada Cataloguing in Publication

Shipley, Jocelyn, author
Shatterproof / Jocelyn Shipley.
(Orca currents)

Issued in print and electronic formats.
ISBN 978-1-4598-1361-8 (paperback).—ISBN 978-1-4598-1362-5 (pdf).—
ISBN 978-1-4598-1363-2 (epub)

I. Title. II. Series: Orca currents
PS8587.H563S53 2016   jc813'.6   c2016-900775-8
                    c2016-900776-6

First published in the United States, 2016
Library of Congress Control Number: 2016931877

Summary: In this high-interest novel for middle readers, thirteen-year-old Nate
gets caught up in a money-making scam based on his resemblance to a celebrity.

*Orca Book Publishers is dedicated to preserving the environment and has
printed this book on Forest Stewardship Council® certified paper.*

Orca Book Publishers gratefully acknowledges the support for its
publishing programs provided by the following agencies: the Government
of Canada through the Canada Book Fund and the Canada Council
for the Arts,and the Province of British Columbia through
the BC Arts Council and the Book Publishing Tax Credit.

Cover photography by Getty Images
Author Photo by Michael Galan

ORCA BOOK PUBLISHERS
www.orcabook.com

Printed and bound in Canada.

19 18 17 16 • 4 3 2 1

Chapter One

Saturday morning I wake up earlier than I do on a school day. I want to leave before I lose my nerve and change my mind. I can't go without checking on Mom, so I poke my head into her room. She's awake but still in bed, tucked under her flowery pink duvet. "Okay, I'm off now," I say, not making eye contact. Not looking at the wheelchair waiting for her. "See you tonight. Love you."

"Bye, love you too." Mom waves and blows me a kiss. "Let me know when you get there. And have a great day!"

I rush to the front door, almost colliding with Etta, Mom's community health worker. "Going for a run?" she asks, stepping aside for me.

I do train most mornings. But not today. "Cross-country meet in Victoria. Coach is driving the team down, then taking us all out for dinner after." It's the same story I told Mom.

But that's not where I'm going.

"Sounds wonderful," Etta says. "You deserve some fun."

I nod, afraid she'll guess I'm lying. "I really wish you were on shift later." Etta is Mom's favorite CHW. But after she gets Mom up and bathed this morning, she will be off for a couple of days.

"Your mom will be fine, just like when you're at school." Etta hangs up her coat and checks her phone. "You're a big help, Nate. She's lucky to have you."

"Thanks. It's just that I'm always here for dinner."

Etta pats my shoulder. "You worry too much. You need to have some fun. Go have a good time."

Guilt almost stops me.

But I can't wait to get out of Herring Bay and off Vancouver Island. I can't wait to see my friend Lug again. I can't wait to hang out like we used to.

I wish I could sleep over at Lug's. Or even stay a couple hours longer. But it's too risky. Sneaking away for one short day will have to be enough.

I jog down our lane and out to the bus stop on the highway. The bus takes me to the ferry terminal. It's going to be expensive, but this day will be so worth it.

As soon as I board the ferry, I rush to line up for the café. The aroma of fried food makes me ravenous. I order bacon, eggs, hash browns and toast, grab a table and devour my feast. Man, it tastes good, especially since I didn't have to make it. I've been doing a lot of cooking since Mom's accident.

Then I find a window seat near the video arcade. I can't waste any money in there, so I plug in my earbuds and listen to music. I drift off to sleep for a while.

When I open my eyes Vancouver is coming into view on the horizon. It looks like a toy city off in the distance. I head out to the deck for some fresh air.

It's a crisp fall day, partly sunny with a light wind. The ocean shines a deep greenish-blue. Fluffy white clouds cap the coastal mountains.

But the closer the ferry sails to the terminal, the worse I feel about leaving Mom today. Yeah, she manages on her own during the week, but when I'm not there, she's lonely. After she broke her back skiing last winter, she lost her job, her busy life and most of her friends. "Nate," she often says, "what would I ever do without you?"

Dad left two weeks after she came home from rehab. He renovated our house to make it accessible for her, and then he moved out. What a jerk!

Actually, he'd started being a jerk before Mom's accident. Maybe he would have left anyway. But his timing sucked. At least he pays for a lot of help for Mom. It made me mad when Mom asked if I'd be seeing him today, since he lives in Victoria. Like I'd want to spend time with him. I haven't talked to my dad since he left. Mom's question also added to my guilt, because she believes I'm going to Victoria.

I hate myself for lying to her. But she forbade me to ever see or talk to

Lug again. And that's not fair. Lug has been my best friend for eight years.

I feel bad about Mom's accident and all, but she can't tell me who to be friends with. If Lug hadn't moved to Vancouver in July, I would be sneaking around behind her back to see him. I'd be forced to lie to her like I'm doing today.

It was such a long, boring summer without Lug. I had nothing to do but help at home with shopping, cooking and cleaning. I had nobody to hang out with except Mom. And she was struggling to adjust to life in a wheelchair and to Dad leaving.

It was way beyond depressing.

Now I've started high school and met some kids. But I don't have any close friends yet. So when Lug texted me to come visit, I said yes.

Then I worked out my fake story for Mom.

She was almost too easy to fool. The idea of me competing at a cross-country meet made her so happy. See, she used to be a track star in high school. She got her degree in phys ed, then worked as a fitness instructor. She even coached my soccer team.

Now she knits. And knits. And knits.

I'm not proud of what I'm doing. But the past seven months have been brutal for me too.

Etta's right. I need to have some fun.

And Lug's the guy to make that happen.

Chapter Two

The ferry docking announcement sounds. I hurry along with the other passengers down the walkway and through the terminal. On the sidewalk outside, I wait for Lug to pick me up as planned.

I text Mom. **Made it to Victoria ok.**

She replies, **Great! Good luck!! Love u!!!**

Half an hour passes. All the other passengers have left on buses or been picked up. Maybe Lug forgot I was coming?

Clouds close in over the sun. Drizzling rain starts. Within minutes it's pouring down full force. I go back inside the terminal to wait.

I'm about to text Lug when a black SUV pulls up. Lug's older sister, Dakota, is driving. She's seventeen and gorgeous. She's also a classic mean girl.

"Thanks for picking me up," I say as I climb into the back beside Lug. It's best to be polite to Dakota. But I don't trust her. She's made Lug's life hell over the years.

"Whatever," she says. "It was the only way I could get to use the car today. If it was my choice, I'd never drive you guys anywhere. Especially to the mall to ogle girls."

"Hey, dude," Lug says. "Good to see ya. Sorry we're late. Dakota had to do her nails."

Dakota does a little finger wave with one hand. Her long nails are painted black. She could probably kill with them.

"No problem," I say.

Dakota doesn't answer, just checks me out in the rearview mirror.

"Don't know how you stand living on the Island," Lug says. "It's way cooler here."

"I know, I know." There's so much more to do in the city. I wish I could come over every weekend. Or at least once a month.

Dakota merges onto the highway. It starts to rain harder. She adjusts the windshield wipers to full speed. Then she glances at me in the rearview mirror again. "Wow, Nate," she says. "You really grew up over the summer."

She's right. I'm way taller. And I'm a lot leaner and more muscular from running. "Um, yeah, I guess," I say.

Is she setting me up?

"You've lost that baby-face thing you had going on," she says. "You look hot."

"Dakota!" Lug says. "Shut up! Don't hit on my friends."

She laughs and signals a lane change. When we're in the fast lane, she flicks her long blond hair over her shoulders. "Seriously, Nate," she says. "Got a girl-friend yet?"

"No." And I'm not discussing girl-friends with Dakota.

"That's hard to believe. You look like the guy on that show, the one about the teen detective."

This must be a setup.

"You know the one," she says, slowing down to exit the highway. "Bo Blaketon? On *Shatterproof*?"

"Oh, please," Lug says. But he takes a long look at me. "Okay, maybe a little bit." Maybe Dakota means it. Because a girl at school told me that too. She seemed surprised when she saw me after the summer. So did a couple other kids.

When we are stopped at a traffic light, Dakota turns around to stare at me. "Yeah, you totally look like Bo Blaketon. Bet you can get a lot of girls now." She sounds serious.

"Dunno." What else can I say?

Dakota turns left onto Seaview Drive. "What I don't know is why you'd want to be seen with Laurence the loser."

Laurence is Lug's real name. But last year Dakota got everybody calling him Lug. It is supposed to be funny because he's stocky and odd-looking. I used to call him Lego Man because he's kind of square shaped with a short neck.

Lug and I both know not to get into it with Dakota. We ignore her and start talking about the games we want to buy.

When Dakota drops us off at West Pacific Mall, she says to me, "See ya, Bo. Have fun picking up girls. And do me a favor? Don't let Laurence be a perv, okay?"

I say, "Thanks again for the ride. Bye."

Lug says, "Hope you crash."

As we head for the entrance I ask him, "So how come it's *Laurence* now?" Trust me, Lug is not a Laurence.

"My sister's just trying to ruin my life," Lug says. "As usual."

At first he hated being called Lug. Then it caught on, and he liked the tough sound of it. That is why Dakota wants to call him Laurence now.

"Yup, that's her goal," I say.

"I still can't believe she ratted us out."

"You," I say. "She ratted you out. I was totally innocent."

Here's what happened. At a beach party after our grad, Lug took photos of some popular girls. They'd changed from their fancy dresses into bikinis and were dancing around the fire. Then he Photoshopped them so it looked like the girls were also smoking and drinking.

Dakota hacked into his iPad and found the photos. She figured out he wanted to make money from them. He was planning to blackmail those girls.

I don't know why he thought that would work. Somebody would have figured out pretty fast that the photos were fake. All I know is that Lug's weird about girls. He's obsessed with them, but he doesn't seem to respect them. I think it comes from the way Dakota treats him.

It turned out that one of the girls was Dakota's best friend's little sister.

So Dakota told her friend. Her friend told their parents. Their parents told Lug's parents. Lug said I was in on it too, so they also told Mom.

Lug's parents convinced everyone to let it go after he proved he'd deleted the photos. They searched his phone, iPad and laptop. He also had to write an apology to the girls. Then his family moved to Vancouver, but that had already been planned.

Mom freaked about the whole thing. I got grounded for two weeks. Which was insanely unfair, because I wasn't in on it.

Okay, I was there when Lug took the photos. But I had no idea what he was planning. See, it was right after Dad left. I was dazed with confusion and rage. All I could think about was myself. How my life had changed.

But Mom said I should have stopped Lug from taking the photos. I should have known he was up to something, because he always is. She said he was a bad influence. She said I couldn't hang out with him. Ever again.

But here I am.

Chapter Three

Our plan is to check out the mall's game and skate stores. Then we'll eat burgers and fries at the food court. Then we'll go to a movie. And then I'll catch another bus and the five o'clock ferry home.

Before we go inside, Lug stops for a cigarette. This is new.

"When did you start smoking?" I ask him.

"Over the summer. Want one?" He offers me the pack.

"No, thanks. I'm training for cross-country."

"So?" He huddles under the entrance overhang. Right beside the *No Smoking Within 10 Meters* sign.

"So it's kind of bad for your lungs." I don't like standing there in the rain with him. "I'll be in the game store."

"Up to you."

I leave him with all the other smokers.

In a few minutes Lug comes to find me. We spend an hour looking at the new games. I can't afford anything. I have just enough money for the bus, ferry and food. It took awhile to save that up.

Lug buys a couple of games he wants. Then we head for the skate shop.

On our way we pass a kiosk full of sunglasses. The upscale ones are locked in glass cases. But the cheaper ones are arranged on spinning racks. Some girls are there, trying them on, giggling and taking selfies.

"Let's check those out," Lug says. I'm not sure if he means the sunglasses or the girls. But whatever, I can look at both.

We circle the kiosk, studying the different styles and sneaking looks at the girls. They sneak looks at us too. Strange. Girls usually ignore us.

"It would be so easy," Lug says.

I pick up a pair of fake designer sunglasses. "What would?" I hope he's not thinking we should try to pick up a couple of those girls.

Lug glances at the sales guy in the booth, who is also watching the girls. Does he think they're hot or that they're going to shoplift? Probably both.

"He's not paying any attention to us," Lug says. "Just grab the ones you want." He starts to slide a pair of sunglasses under his hoodie.

I have to stop him. We can't get into trouble. "Hey, over here?" I call to the sales guy. "How much are these?" I hold up a random pair of sunglasses.

The sales guy comes out of the kiosk to take a closer look.

Lug puts the sunglasses he was going to steal back on the rack.

"Twenty bucks," the sales guy says, keeping one eye on the girls. "It says right here on the tag."

"Too much," I say.

He shrugs. "Two for thirty-five."

"Still too much. But thanks anyway."

We hurry away. When we're out of the sales guy's hearing, Lug says, "Thanks a lot, man. You almost got me busted."

"Exactly. You can afford those. You don't have to steal them."

"I know. But it's the challenge."

"Well, guess what? I don't need the challenge of my mom getting a call from security at West Pacific Mall."

"Does she even know you're here?"

"No, and she can't find out." We walk on in silence. I'd forgotten how Lug is always up to something. And how that something usually gets him in trouble. Gets *us* in trouble.

"Excuse me?" a soft voice says. We both turn to see the group of girls from the kiosk following us.

Lug's eyes light up. "Well, hello there. How can we help you lovely ladies?"

I cringe. Doesn't he know how fake he sounds? How pathetic?

The girls eye me like I'm a superhero or something. "This might sound crazy," one of them says to me, "but we were just wondering."

"You were?" I ask. She looks perfect. Tight jeans, funky boots, long shiny black hair. "Wondering what?"

She blushes and can't speak. Her friends urge her on. "Okay," she finally says.

"Here goes. Are you, um, are you Bo Blaketon?"

"What?"

"Are you Bo Blaketon? You know, from *Shatterproof*?"

Whoa. How I wish I was.

I glance over at Lug. His eyebrows have shot way up, and his mouth hangs wide-open. He's probably thinking what I am. This is too weird. Dakota said the same thing in the car.

"Yeah, I know that show," I say. "But no, sorry, I'm not him."

The girl tilts her head and squints at me. "Are you sure?"

I snort. "Last time I checked."

"Oh, come on," she says. "You're him. But don't worry—we won't invade your privacy."

"No, really, I'm not."

She gives me a flirty smile and fluffs her hair. "I heard that *Shatterproof* is filming in North Van next week."

"So?"

"So that's why you're in town. And you're from here, so it all makes perfect sense."

"Well, it would if I was Bo Blaketon. But I'm not."

The girl touches my arm gently. It feels like an electric shock. "It's okay," she says. "We won't announce it to the whole world. But can you get me on your show?"

"No way!"

"So you are him!"

"No, I meant I can't get you on that show. Because I'm not Bo Blaketon."

"Oh, please?" She actually flutters her eyelashes and pouts her lips. "Just as an extra?"

Lug butts in. "Hey, he might be able to make that happen."

I frown and shake my head at him. "What are you doing?"

"He-he," Lug says. "Can't blame these pretty things for trying."

"But I'm not Bo Blaketon!"

They all stare at me like I'm lying. Even Lug.

"Let's go." I stride away. "This is ridiculous."

The girl follows, her friends behind her. "Look, I'm sorry," she says. "I should have respected your privacy. But can you please just sign my arm?" She pulls a purple marker out of her purse. "Then I promise I'll leave you alone."

She's wearing a flowery shirt, open over a tank top. She slips one sleeve off. Thrusts her shoulder at me. Points at her bicep. "Here," she says. "Please?" She hands me the marker.

I can't not take it. And then I'm scrawling on her smooth skin *Bo B*. It kind of looks like *BoB*, which makes me laugh. It's a nervous laugh though. What was I thinking?

"Omigod!" She actually starts to cry. "Thank you so much!"

Her friends gather close to take pictures. Lug steps in and shields my face with his hand. "Ladies, please! Privacy!"

The girl wipes her tears and grabs her marker back. "If you change your mind about me being an extra, here's my number." She writes it on my hand.

"Sorry, but we have to go." I pull Lug away with me.

The other girls call after us, "Hey, Bo, come back! Sign us too!"

I break into a run.

Chapter Four

When Lug catches up with me he says, "What the what, dude? That was brilliant!"

"That was wrong!" I can't believe I did that. I think I might throw up. I should go back and find that girl. Tell her the truth.

But then we enter RadRide, and I'm totally distracted. It's the best store on the planet. You used to have to go to the States to shop at one. But they've finally opened a store here in Vancouver. I hope they open one on the Island soon.

They've got longboards, cruisers— every kind of skateboard. They even have kits and parts to custom-build your own. Plus they carry all the coolest brands of clothes, shoes and accessories.

I want everything!

For a while I'm overwhelmed with looking at the stock. So is Lug. We don't talk. We just sigh and drool.

And then I see it.

A Globe Bantam Galaxy Cruiser. Black with an orange-and-green-and-blue-universe print. Gradual kickboard. Simple but sweet!

Lug notices me admiring it. "You like?"

"Oh yeah."

"Better than that chick whose arm you just signed?" He points to my hand, where she wrote her number. I stick my hand in my pocket. I need to go scrub that off as soon as we're done in here.

"Yup. She was just some girl. But this is my dream board."

"So buy it."

"I wish! It's ninety-five bucks. Can't afford it."

"That sucks." Lug studies sets of wheels. "Hey, why don't you ask your old man? He's loaded, right?"

"You've got to be kidding." Lug knows what happened with my parents. He knows how pissed off I am at my dad.

"So he's a jerk. You can still spend his money."

I think about that for a minute. It might be satisfying. I could pretend I want to see him, then change my mind once he buys me the board. "Nah. I'd have to actually speak to him."

"Okay, I get it," Lug says. "How about this? That girl wanting to be an extra on *Shatterproof* gave me an idea."

Uh-oh. Lug's ideas always end badly. "I don't like the sound of this."

"Just listen, okay? You pretend to be that Bo Blaketon guy, and we sign girls up to be extras for the *Shatterproof* shoot next week. They pay us twenty bucks each up front. For their application, like a registration fee."

The way Lug's mind works kills me. "And we'd get their phone numbers too?"

"No, we'd just ask for an email address. So it wouldn't sound like we're hitting on them or anything. It has to seem legit." He smirks. "But if they want to give us their numbers, we'd be okay with that."

"And why would they believe us?"

"Because all girls want to be on TV." Lug runs his hand over the Globe Bantam

Galaxy Cruiser's deck. "Nice," he says. "Can't you just see yourself on this?"

"No, because I can't afford it."

"Then let's try my plan."

"No, thanks." I can't do that. "Sure, girls might give us money," I say. "But it would be a crime. We'd be committing fraud."

"Don't be such a wimp."

"But what if we get caught? Like I said earlier, I don't want my mom getting a call from security."

"We won't get caught," Lug says. "If you can fool Dakota, you can fool anyone."

"But I didn't fool Dakota. She just said I kind of looked like Bo Blaketon. Not that she thought I was him."

"Still," Lug says. "Those girls thought you were."

I check around the store to make sure those girls aren't in here. Then I take another look at the wall of shoes.

There's a pair of Vans I'd love. "That's because they wanted to believe they were meeting a celebrity."

"So we let them have their wish. We let them enjoy a fantasy that they're going to be discovered. We'd be doing them a favor."

"I don't care. I'm so not doing this."

"C'mon, *Bo*," Lug says. "You could make enough in an hour to buy that board."

"I don't want it that bad."

"You know you do."

He's right. I do. But I'm not scamming girls. Mom would go nuts. "Forget it," I say. "I'll ask my dad for the money."

I take out my phone to call him. I'm hoping he'll be so happy to hear from me that he'll say yes. He might even ask what else I need from RadRide.

My dad answers right away. "Nate!" he says. "Good to hear from you! What's up?"

The sound of his voice almost makes me cry.

I hate him so much.

But I miss him too. It's confusing.

"Um, hey, Dad," I say. "How's it going?"

"Great. I'd really like to see you. Would you consider coming down for a weekend? Even a day? Jewel would like that too. She's eager to meet you."

Someday I might agree to see my dad. But I want nothing to do with Jewel, the hot young TV weather girl he's dating. "Maybe," I say. "So anyway, I'm in this skate store? And there's this board I really want. And since you missed my birthday and all, I was wondering if you could call the store and give them your credit-card number?"

Silence. Then my dad says, "I'd be happy to work out a financial arrangement for you, Nate. But I have to run it by your mom first."

"Why?"

"Because I don't want her to accuse me of trying to buy your affection."

He's right. That's exactly what she'd think. "Oh, I'm sure she wouldn't mind."

"And I'm sure she would. Where are you anyway?"

I name a mall in Victoria, just in case he tells Mom I called.

"Really? Let's meet for lunch. I could be there in twenty minutes."

"Sorry, but I'm with the cross-country team. We have a meet this afternoon. We just stopped in here for some snacks."

"Where's your meet? I'll come see you there."

"Bye, Dad."

I feel like crap after I end the call. It hurts so much that he left us. I take another look at that board. "Okay," I tell Lug. "We'll ask one girl to sign up and see how it goes."

Chapter Five

"You won't regret it," Lug says as we leave RadRide. "It's gonna be easy money."

Something tells me that I *will* regret it. Big-time. "Yeah, but it's still a scam."

"Too right. It's a *Shatterproof* scam!"

I groan. "Maybe we shouldn't do this," I say.

"Hey, if girls are stupid enough to believe us, that's their problem. Not ours."

"I guess." I'm so conflicted. I want the money. But I know it's wrong. "What if we take money some girl really needs?"

"Needs for what?"

"I don't know." I think of all the stuff I need money for. "Like maybe bus fare, school lunches and trips?"

Lug veers right to avoid a mom pushing a double stroller. "Girls who shop here are rich. What's twenty bucks to them? A pair of earrings or new nail polish? A couple fancy lattes and some cupcakes? Big deal."

We make our way along the crowded mall. When we reach the food court, I say, "Let's get lunch first." The aroma of burgers and fries and pizza is hard to resist. And maybe food will distract Lug from his plan.

"Nah, let's eat later." Lug steers me past the fast-food places.

I could refuse. I could say I'm starving and I'll catch up with him after I eat.

But part of me wants to see if we can actually do it. Signing that girl's arm was a rush. I need a little adventure in my life. "So how's it going to work?" I ask. "Shouldn't we have ID or clipboards or something?"

"Definitely." He stops and takes his iPad from his backpack. "Check this out."

He's made a document that looks official. The "Extras Needed" page even has the *Shatterproof* logo. "Jeez, Lug! When did you do that?"

"While you were talking to your dad."

"You're evil, you know that?"

"Know it and proud of it."

We walk on until we get to a store called Marlena's. It's full of all kinds of girly accessories. Everything in the window is pastel and sparkly.

Two girls come out with bulging shopping bags, checking their phones. One is blond, the other a redhead. They're both hot.

"Hey, there," Lug says. They ignore him and keep walking.

"Want to be on TV?"

They stop, turn and give him their full attention. "Omigod! Yes!" the blonde squeals. "When? How?"

"This is Bo Blaketon," Lug says, pointing to me. "And I'm Laurence, his personal assistant. We're here today to find extras for an episode of Bo's show *Shatterproof*. We're filming in North Van next week."

I nod at the girls and try to smile like a star. But inside I'm shaking. What if they realize I'm not Bo Blaketon?

"Omigod! Omigod! Omigod!" the redhead shrieks. "I love that show!"

"Me too! How do we sign up?" the blonde asks.

Lug holds out his iPad. "I just need your email addresses," he says, "so we can send you the times and locations."

"Seriously?" The girls hesitate. The redhead says, "Don't we have to like, audition or something?"

"No, no. Not to be extras." Lug taps on his screen, like he's searching for information. "It's a two-part episode, and some of it takes place at a concert."

He shows them the screen. I peer over his shoulder and see that he's opened the official website for the show. There's a notice about the shooting in North Van next weekend, but nothing about extras. Or about us scouting at the mall. But the girls don't even bother to look.

"So that's it?" the blonde says. "We just give you our contact info?"

"That's it." Lug brings the "Extras" page he made back up. "Oh, and I should tell you that there's a twenty-dollar processing fee for your application. But don't worry, you'll make that back in your first hour. And we'll need you on set for several hours. So you stand to make good money. Paid in cash at the end of the day."

"What about school?" the redhead says.

"Not a problem," Lug says. "We're filming on the weekend. And if you know anybody else who might be interested, please let them know. We need lots of different looks. Lots of diversity."

The blonde is already getting her money out. She hands Lug a twenty.

"Thanks," he says. "I'll email you a receipt tonight. And the rest of the info will come in a few days." He holds out the iPad for her to enter her details. "There'll also be a permission form and liability waiver for your parent or guardian to sign, scan and return."

He eyes them up and down. "Unless, of course, you're both eighteen?"

The redhead giggles and shakes her head. "Thirteen," she says.

"We should call Tenshi and Carlotta and Violet," the blonde says. "They'd love this." She pulls out her phone. "How long are you going to be here, Laurence?"

"Only for another hour, so your friends better hurry."

"And what about guys? Can they be extras too?"

Lug pulls a sad look. "No, sorry. Bo has a lot of friends from when he went to school here. He wants to use them."

The redhead pays him and enters her details on his iPad. Then she turns to me. "Can I take a selfie with you?" she asks. "And can I have your autograph?"

Lug steps between us fast, like he's my bodyguard. "Sorry," he says. "Not now. We don't want everybody in the mall to figure out Bo's here and mob him. We're trying to keep things low-key while we find our extras. But there will be chances for photos and autographs on set."

"Oh," she says. "Well, okay then. See you guys next weekend!"

We stand there in shock as the girls stroll away.

"Wow!" Lug says. "That was awesome! Even easier than I thought."

I have no words. I feel terrible.

But I also feel excited. That was an even bigger rush than the girl writing her number on my hand. They actually paid us twenty bucks each!

When I can finally speak, I say, "Good thing you stopped her from taking my picture."

"Yeah, we'll have to be careful there's no evidence."

Yikes! Why didn't I think of that sooner? My face could be all over social media if some girl gets a photo. "That's for sure. I don't want the real Bo Blaketon to see me online, pretending to be him."

"Told you I had it all figured out. We'll stick to no photos until the shoot. And oh, look at that." Lug points toward the door of Marlena's. "There's our next forty bucks."

Chapter Six

The two girls who come out of Marlena's are just as pretty as the first ones. And just as easy to con. As soon as Lug mentions being on TV, they're into it. They don't ask questions. They just do that "omigod, omigod, omigod" thing. And then they pay us and sign up.

Lug reels the girls in with his great spiel. He handles everything like a pro.

He stops them from taking photos and whisks the money out of sight. We don't want mall security to start asking questions.

I stop being nervous and start to enjoy myself. No girl has ever looked at me like these ones do. I feel all mellow but also strong and powerful, like after I've run ten κ. I could get used to being Bo Blaketon!

That makes me think of my dad. He used to host a radio talk show. Is this how he felt when he was a local celebrity? Like everything he said was important? Like everything he did was special?

Thinking of my dad snaps me back to reality. I don't want to be like him.

I don't want to be a jerk.

Scamming these girls is evil. So as soon as we've signed up enough for me to buy that board, I tell Lug, "That's it. I'm going for lunch."

Lug doesn't try to stop me. All the way to the food court he blabs on about how great this is and how rich we're going to be.

I find us a table at the edge of the food court, way back by the washrooms. I don't want anybody else thinking they know me from TV. I don't want Lug trying to sign up more girls. I just want to eat my burger in peace.

But first I go scrub that girl's number off my hand. I find a beanie in my backpack and put it on. Then I keep my head down. I don't look at anybody. I don't look around at all.

After we've got our food, Lug pulls out his wallet. He counts off six twenties for me. "Your pay," he says. "Man, I make a great assistant, don't I?"

I hide the money in my wallet fast. "Yup. But you can take the rest of the day off."

"What?"

I slather some ketchup on my fries. "We're going to a movie, remember? And I'm done being Bo Blaketon."

"No way," he says. "We can make another hundred or more each, no sweat."

"I've got enough for that board. Plus tax. I'm good."

"Nate, you're not thinking straight. We've got a great thing going. Who wants to go see a movie when we can make this kind of cash?"

"Actually, I am thinking straight. Forget the movie. I'm going to go buy that board and get out of here. Before we get caught."

"No, you're not. Would Bo Blaketon be carrying a skateboard when he's signing up extras?"

"But he's not signing up any more extras. He's stopping now. You know, quit while you're ahead."

Lug finishes the last of his fries. "I don't think so."

"What if some of those girls go home and tell their parents about being an extra? Their parents will know we scammed their daughters."

"Trust me, they won't. Those girls are all still at the mall. Probably buying new outfits to wear on set."

He could be right. But still. "What if one of them did get a picture of me as Bo Blaketon and she posts it somewhere? What if the real Bo Blaketon sees it and calls his people? And they call the cops?"

"Look," he says. "You're right. That might happen. But not in the next couple of hours. And after that we'll be gone, and they'll never find us."

I slurp down my soda and pile our used dishes onto a tray. "I just don't feel right about it."

Lug bursts out laughing. "Not one of those girls asked us for ID. Not one of them called her parents to get permission.

Not one of them checked on our story at all. It's their own fault if we take their money."

Before I can answer, my phone vibrates. There's a text from Mom. I read it and cringe.

"Great," I tell Lug. "My dad called my mom, and she wants to know what's going on. Why I asked him for money."

"Parents," Lug says with a shake of his head. "Always in your face."

I text Mom back. **Just had lunch. Have to go stretch b4 race.**

I don't answer her question about Dad. I'll have to talk my way out of why I asked him for money later.

I leave Lug to finish his drink and carry our trays to the bin. I take my time sorting out garbage from what goes in recycling.

I can't help thinking about all the times Lug's schemes have gotten me in trouble. And how mad and disappointed

Mom would be if she ever found out about today.

That's it. Our scam has to end.

When I come back to the table I tell Lug, "I'm going to go buy that board. Then I'm going to the skate park until it's time to get the bus to the ferry."

"You can't bail on me now."

"And who's gonna stop me? You gonna beat me up right here?"

"Oh, no need for violence," Lug says. "I'll just let your mom know what you've been doing."

Chapter Seven

Lug pulls out his phone. "I'm sure your mom would love to hear how much money you made scamming innocent girls."

My heart skips a beat. "You wouldn't!"

"Oh yeah?" Lug starts tapping at the screen. "Try me."

I can't let him call Mom. I stop his hand and say, "Okay, okay, let's talk about this. Remember how much trouble I got in after that thing you did at grad?"

"That thing I did? You were there too, dude."

I nod in agreement. "I know. But you took the photos. You Photoshopped them. You were the one planning to blackmail those girls."

"And your point is?" Lug picks up his drink and stirs the ice with his straw.

How do I say this so he won't think I'm blaming him? "Okay, yeah, I'm guilty too, but my mom's got enough trouble, with her accident and my dad leaving and everything. She doesn't need this." I can still see Mom's face the day she got the phone call from that girl's parents. Shock. Anger. Disappointment.

I tried to explain that it wasn't my idea. I promised never to see Lug again.

But I broke my word. And now I'm in too deep.

"Huh," Lug says. "I do feel sorry for your mom. But I feel way sorrier for you."

"Wait. What?"

"Because you used to be a lot more fun," Lug says. "The old Nate would want to sign up more girls."

"Yeah? Well, the old Lug wouldn't threaten to call my mom."

Lug makes a face at me, but he puts his phone away.

"Thanks, man," I say. "Seriously."

"Whatever. But you're boring now, you know that?"

Before I can defend myself, this little kid races by our table. He's maybe three or four. There's a girl about our age right behind him. She's calling, "Tree! Stop right now!"

The kid laughs like a maniac and zooms away. He dodges between the crowded tables. Because he's small, he can squeeze through where she can't.

"Tree!" She sounds desperate. "Get back here!"

Of course he doesn't listen. He circles around and around, always just out of reach.

Nobody bothers to help her. Nobody pays any attention at all.

So the next time the kid passes our table, I'm ready. I stick out my arm and grab him. "Hey, little buddy," I say as he struggles to get free. "Where you going so fast?"

The girl catches up and takes him from me. "Oh, thank you, thank you, thank you," she says. "I'd be in so much trouble if I lost him at the mall."

She kneels down to scold him. "Tree! You know Dad told you to stay with me all the time!"

He scowls and shrieks, "Ice cream! Want ice cream!"

"We're not getting ice cream." She holds out a plastic baggie of mini carrots.

"We're supposed to have veggies for snacks."

"No! Want crackers."

She sighs and pulls a baggie of Goldfish crackers from her purse. "Fine. Here."

Tree climbs onto a chair beside Lug to eat them.

"Sorry," the girl says. "Do you mind if he sits there? I don't see any free tables."

"No problem," Lug says. "You can join us too."

The girl straightens up and says, "Thanks! And thanks again for the help." She's wearing this weird sweater that looks like it's made from other sweaters. And a jean skirt that looks like it's made from old jeans.

"You're welcome," I say. "He's a pretty fast kid!"

Lug stares at her. At first I think he's wondering how to ask if she wants to be an extra. But then I notice he's scowling.

And then I notice that one side of her face is scarred. It looks like a birthmark or a bad burn. But it's partly hidden by her long curly hair, so I can't tell for sure.

"I'm Spring," she says. "And I guess you know my little brother is Tree."

I laugh. She has this sweet but confident vibe. "Yeah, I heard."

"And you are?"

"Me? Oh, I'm uh—"

"He's Bo Blaketon!" Lug says. "And I'm his assistant, Laurence."

He waits. But she doesn't react like the other girls did. She doesn't gasp, giggle, burst into tears or scream.

"What?" Lug says. "Don't you recognize him?"

Spring takes a good long look at me. "I don't think so. Should I?"

"*Shatterproof?*" Lug says. "You know, the TV show?"

"Oh," she says. "Sorry, no. We don't have a TV. My parents don't believe in it."

"Really? They're like, religious or something?" Lug asks.

"They're homeschoolers."

"So you don't go to school?"

"My dad teaches us at home. He follows the provincial curriculum." Spring sounds like she's had to defend homeschooling before. "Plus we do a lot of enrichment activities and field trips."

"Sucks that you can't watch TV though," Lug says. "But hey, the first season of *Shatterproof* is on Netflix. You get that?"

"Yeah, but I'm only allowed to watch nature shows or educational stuff." Spring gazes at me again. "But I'd like to watch *Shatterproof*."

"Oh, you'd love it," Lug says. "It's about this teen detective, who's played by my man Bo here."

"Wow! A real TV star!" Spring finger-combs her hair so it covers more of her face. "But what are you doing at the mall?"

"Glad you asked!" Lug launches into his sales pitch. He sounds so professional, I almost believe him. No wonder all those girls signed up without asking questions.

Spring takes the empty cracker bag from Tree as she listens. "That's so amazing," she says, brushing crumbs from Tree's mouth. "But I don't have twenty bucks."

Lug sputters with disbelief. "Everybody has twenty bucks."

"No they don't," I say. "Lots of people don't."

"Hey, I wish I did. I'd love to be an extra on your show," Spring says.

Lug pulls the sad face he used when that girl asked if guys could sign up. "That's too bad. But we do need the registration fee."

"No we don't," I say. "We could let her sign up for free, and then she could pay it back from her earnings."

"Seriously?" Spring's face lights up. "You'd let me do that?"

"Do that?" Tree says.

Lug gives me a dirty look. "Aw, no, so sorry. We can't waive the fee."

"Sure we can. No big deal." I push Lug's iPad toward her. "Just enter your name and contact info. We'll do the rest."

Chapter Eight

Just as Spring is finished entering her details, Tree jumps down from the table. "Peepee!" he shouts.

"Oops, sorry. I'll be right back." Spring grabs Tree in her arms and races him to the washroom.

Lug squashes his empty drink cup with his fist. "Jeez, man. Why'd you do that?"

"Do what?"

"Sign her up for free!"

I lean back and cross my arms over my chest. "Because she didn't have the money."

"Exactly. And now we'll never get that twenty bucks!"

"And she'll never get to be an extra. This whole thing is fake, remember?"

"So?" Lug throws his squashed cup toward the garbage bin. He misses.

I go and put it in the bin. When I come back I say, "So I wanted her contact info."

He gasps. "You're joking, right?"

"Why would I be joking?"

"Did you see that scar?"

I look him right in the eye. "What about it?"

Lug shakes his head with disgust. "No wonder her parents took her out of school."

I want to hit him. But he's way bigger and heavier than I am. And we're in a public place. "Not necessarily. Some parents just don't like the school system."

"Yeah, because their ugly kid would get bullied to death. She's a freak."

"No, she's not. She's a pretty girl with a scar of some kind."

"And here comes Freakface now." Lug stands to leave the table. "I'm going for a smoke."

Spring is holding Tree's hand like she's scared he might escape again. "Your assistant's leaving?"

"He had to, um, make some calls." I mimic smoking. "Hey, you guys want a drink or something? I mean, if you're not busy?"

"Ice cream!" Tree says.

"That would be great," Spring says.

We go over to the ice-cream place and order sundaes. I use some of the money I was saving for dinner on the ferry. I don't want to spend what I made pretending to be Bo Blaketon. Luckily, nobody asks if I'm him.

As we wait for our order, I wonder how I could give that money back.

I'd like to reverse this whole day. I have a feeling if Spring ever finds out we were running a scam, she'll hate me.

And I really, really want her to like me.

We carry our sundaes to a table. Spring tucks a napkin bib on Tree and says, "This is turning out to be a great field trip, right, Tree?"

"Ice cream," he says as he digs in.

I stir my chocolate sauce. "Field trip?"

"That's what we call it. My dad had a meeting today, my mom's working, and my other brothers are at soccer, so normally we'd be at the park. But because it's so rainy, my dad dropped us off here. There's a play area, and Tree can run around. Or run away from me." She smiles and eats some of her sundae. "This is so good," she says. "But anyway, my dad calls it a field trip so he'll feel better about us spending a Saturday here. I'm supposed to be researching consumerism, so it's a learning experience."

"And what have you learned?"

"What I already knew. That the mall is full of overpriced junk nobody needs."

"I know, right?" I think about that Globe Bantam Galaxy Cruiser. It's not junk, but I know I don't need it. What I need is to find a way out of this mess. "Do you ever want to go to regular school?"

"Sometimes," she says. "I think I will for high school next year." She fiddles with her hair, twisting it into a loose braid. Then she lets it fall back over her scar.

"So what happened?"

"Why am I homeschooled?"

"Yeah, but I meant about your face." Mom's told me how hard it is when people turn away rather than ask about her wheelchair. Or when they just look at her with pity. Or when they don't look at her at all.

"Really? Nobody ever asks. It scares people."

"I'm asking. That's a pretty impressive scar."

"Okay." Spring helps Tree scoop up the last of his sundae. "It happened at the homeschoolers' summer barbecue two years ago. I was toasting a marshmallow over a campfire. It started to fall off the stick, so I reached in to push it back on. And then my hair caught fire."

"Whoa! That's scary!"

"Yeah, it was. Hair products are extremely flammable." She pushes her hair back so I can get a good look at her scar.

It's red and shiny and scaly. It stretches from her chin up to her hairline, very close to her eye. I try not to act grossed out like Lug did. "Must be painful," I say. "I'm so sorry that happened to you."

"So am I," she says. "But I'm so lucky and grateful that I didn't lose my eye. And yeah, it hurt a lot."

I want to tell her about Mom's accident. How it changed everything. But I don't know where to start. While I'm trying to find the words, Spring keeps talking.

"I've had a lot of plastic surgery, and I'll have more as I grow. So what you see isn't the final version. This is just a temporary scar."

She gives a bitter laugh. "Of course, my parents turned it into a learning experience. So, like, I've learned that true beauty is internal. I've learned how superficial people can be. I've learned to say, *If you don't like how I look, step off!*"

She eats the last bite of her sundae and licks the spoon. "And now I've learned that even with my freaky face, I can still be on TV! How cool is that?"

Chapter Nine

Spring's words make me want to throw up.

What have I done?

If we don't contact her next week, will she think it's because of her scar? Will she think we were just being nice, letting her sign up for free? That we never meant to let her be on camera?

Maybe I could tell her the episode got canceled? But the real shoot is happening next week in North Van. What if she hears about it and goes there looking for me? I have to think of something fast.

"About the TV thing," I say. "Are you sure your parents will be okay with it? I mean, if you're not allowed to watch TV, why would they let you be an extra?"

"Because I'll present it as a learning experience," she says. "I have to do a major research project. An inside look at the TV industry is perfect. I can research and evaluate how it all works. How a series is made."

"Oh." There goes that escape route. "Yeah, I guess it could be educational."

"My parents will love it!" She wipes chocolate sauce from Tree's face. "So any inside information you can give me would be helpful, Bo. Could I interview you?"

"Um, yeah, maybe." I haven't finished my sundae, and now I can't. This is getting worse and worse. Did I just say maybe she could interview me? As Bo Blaketon?

"Oh, thank you! That would be so cool. You being the star and all." She frowns at the melting pool of my sundae. "You didn't like it?"

"I had a big lunch. Guess I should have ordered small instead of large."

"Hey, we could do the interview right now. Because I know you must be busy, and we might not find another time."

Luckily, Tree jumps down from the table and shouts, "Play!"

Spring catches him in a bear hug. "Okay, Treester." Then she says to me, "Maybe this is not a good time for an interview after all."

"Rain check," I say. Because I do want to talk to her again. But not as

Bo Blaketon. Just as me. As for how I'm going to manage that, I've no clue.

And then Lug returns. He eyes our sundae dishes. "Nice meeting you," he says to Spring. "But we have to get back to work now. Bo is a busy man." He turns and walks away, beckoning me to come along.

"We'll walk with you," Spring says, grabbing Tree's hand. "If that's okay. We have some time to kill until my dad picks us up."

"Of course," I say. We clear our table and follow Lug.

"Are you off to rehearsal or something?" Spring asks. "Or are you still signing up extras?"

"Laurence wants a few more names," I say. "In case some kids change their minds. Or can't make the times. Always better to have a wait list. You know, people we can call on short notice if somebody doesn't show up."

What am I talking about? I've no idea how extras are hired. I'm just digging myself in deeper.

"Oh, I'm getting so excited about this!" Spring says. "I'm going to do a super project. And honestly, the idea of being on TV is so awesome. Before my accident, I did a lot of theater. I went to drama camp in the summer, and I had some roles in VanCityKids Productions."

"Cool," I say. "You'd be good onstage."

She guides Tree out of the way of an elderly man with a walker. "Thanks. But I haven't had a part since then." With her free hand she arranges her hair over her scar. "I don't like to think it's because of how I look, but it's hard not to."

"That's so not fair!" I say. Right. And it's also not fair that I pretended to sign her up as an extra.

"Life's not fair," she says. "I've learned that lesson well." She stops to let Tree look in the window of a toy store. "I should be taking notes," she says. "The price of toys, where they're made, whether they encourage creative play or are just Hollywood merchandise."

Tree wants everything in the window. He wants to go into the store. "Sorry, no deal," Spring says, pulling him away. "You've got lots of nice toys at home, Treeling." He bursts into tears.

As we walk on, she says over Tree's sobbing, "I know everything is over-priced and probably made by child labor. But I get how much he wants the stuff he sees." She holds out her free arm to show off her patched sweater. "See, I made this from old sweaters, and I totally believe in recycling and all, but sometimes I want something brand new and in style. Like everybody else has."

"I get that." Being in this mall has made me want all kinds of stuff I don't need. That Globe Bantam Cruiser, the latest games, the most expensive brands of clothes and shoes. "Commercialism sucks."

"Yeah, it does. But it creates jobs, so it's not all bad. And now that I'm going to make good money being an extra, I can buy myself some trendy clothes. My parents can't object if I pay for them myself. How much do you think I'll make?"

"Hard to say." Impossible to tell her she's not going to make any money. She looks so thrilled, I just can't. "Enough for some new clothes for sure."

"I won't spend it all on clothes though. I'll donate some to charity too."

I'm such a horrible person, leading her on. But I say, "That's so nice of you."

Tree has stopped crying. He sees the play area ahead and tugs hard on

Spring's hand. "I better let him loose for a bit," Spring says. "Catch up with you later?"

"We'll be at that girly store," I call as she chases after Tree.

I like this girl. I really, really like her. I have to tell her I'm not Bo Blaketon.

But how?

Chapter Ten

I head down the mall, looking for Lug. He's waiting for me outside RadRide. "Glad you got rid of Freakface and the brat," he says. "They're bad for business."

I don't answer. I hope Spring heard me say where we'd be. Because I have to talk to her again. I have to confess. Today. In person.

Lug points at the window display. "Once we've signed up more girls, you'll be able to get that board and those Vans."

I stare in the window and feel like the slimeball I am. Before today I was happy with my shabby sneakers. I was happy with my beat-up old longboard at home. But as soon as I went in RadRide, I wanted more. "I don't think so."

"Sure you will," Lug says. "You could even afford a new shirt."

"No, I mean I've changed my mind. I don't want that stuff anymore."

Lug starts walking away. "Oh, I get it. You're feeling guilty for scamming Freakface."

He's right. I am. "Don't call her that."

"Just saying. You could do way better, man."

"Don't say that either."

We move along in silence. I have to think of a way out of this mess.

How can I tell Spring who I really am?

Maybe I can say the mall made me crazy. Made me want money just like she does. That's a normal teenage thing, right? To want cool stuff? To want what everybody else has? And that made me make a bad choice. That made me pretend to be a TV star.

"I'm done," I finally tell Lug. "I'm going to tell Spring the truth." I have to. I want to see her again. But just as myself.

"No way," Lug says. "Not until we've made another couple hundred. Then you can tell Freakface whatever you want."

"Shut up!" I punch Lug's shoulder. Hard.

"Hey, that hurt!" But instead of punching me back, he says, "Okay. I didn't want to do this, but you give me no choice." He pushes me out of the flow of shoppers. We stop by an information sign.

He pulls his iPad out of his backpack. He boots it up and shows me the screen.

I see and hear myself pretending to be Bo Blaketon. I see girls giving me money.

Holy crap! I'm screwed!

Mostly Lug took the money, acting as my assistant. But a few times he said they should give it to me. That must be when he took these.

And then I see something worse. He's also got a video of me signing that girl's arm as Bo Blaketon. "You idiot! We said no pictures."

"No, we said the girls couldn't take pictures. We never said I couldn't."

How did I not notice what he was doing? I guess I wasn't really paying attention. Because I never thought my best friend would do that. Apparently he cares more about money than he does about me.

"You have to delete those," I say.

"They're insurance."

"Don't even think about sending those to my parents."

Lug laughs. "I wasn't planning to. I'm going to post them on YouTube. For Bo Blaketon and his fans to see. Oh, and I'm sure Freakface will be interested too."

I grab for his iPad. But he was expecting that and holds on tight. "Relax," he says. "You help me sign ten more girls, and I'll delete the videos."

Should I trust him to keep his word? Probably not. But what else can I do?

I mean, I could face telling Spring the truth. I'd find some way to make her forgive me. But if those go online, I'm dead. "I can't believe you'd do that to me," I say. "That's way worse than telling my mom. The whole world will know, and I could get into serious trouble. I could get charged with fraud or something."

Lug shrugs and says, "Yup."

"Fine," I say. "But then it's over. And we're not friends anymore."

"Hey, man. That's harsh."

"Well, it's on you. Friends don't blackmail friends." I remember all the trouble he's gotten me into over the years. I remember when we were ten and Lug held me underwater at the beach. He thought it was funny, but I almost drowned. And I remember how Mom didn't want me to hang out with him anymore after the grad-party photo incident.

Maybe she was right.

We reach the store called Marlena's, where we found all the girls this morning. Lug sits on a nearby bench to wait for prey. I stand as far from him as possible, scanning the folks in the mall. What if Spring can't find us?

But in a few minutes she and Tree come along. They make quite a pair. She's definitely noticeable with her handmade clothes, amazing hair and brutal scar. And Tree actually looks a bit like a sapling. He's skinny, with long arms and legs. His head seems over-sized because of all his thick, curly hair.

Hair the same chestnut brown as Spring's. Hair that makes you want to touch it. "Hey, guys," I say. "You found us."

Lug gives them a fake smile. Then he's on his feet as two girls who aren't exactly pretty exit the store. "Hello there," he says. "Do you beauties like *Shatterproof*?" He launches into his sales pitch, and they're hooked.

Except this time, Spring reels them in. She ignores the *go away* look Lug gives her and says, "I just signed up. And I'm so thrilled that Bo wants his show to be inclusive and diverse."

They can't wait to hand her their money. They even pretend they don't see her scar.

I can't believe she's getting involved. I watch carefully to make sure Lug isn't taking any more videos. I don't want Spring to get in trouble because of me.

Chapter Eleven

My phone vibrates with another text from Mom. **How's it going? Any updates?**

I have to reply or she'll get worried. So I say, **Race starting. Will b in touch later.**

Then I turn my phone off. It hits me that I don't care anymore if Mom finds out about today. I know she'll be mad, but I'll just have to deal with that.

What I don't know is how Spring will react. From what I've seen so far, I'm pretty sure she's going to be super angry. And that's what I really care about.

"What time is your dad picking you up?" I ask her. I hope it's not too soon. Because I can't tell her the truth until Lug has made as much money as he wants. And after that, it's going to take some time to explain. Which is going to be tricky because I have to catch my bus by four to make it to the ferry in time.

"Four o'clock," she says. "But I might call and beg him to pick us up now."

"Please don't go yet." I need more time to tell her.

"I'd really like to stay," she says. "But I don't think Tree's going to last." We watch him climb around on the bench by the store. Then he jumps off, pretending to fly. She pulls out her phone and starts texting. "I don't want him to get wild and run away again."

"Yeah, I see what you mean." Okay, this is it. I can't keep lying to her. I don't care what Lug says or does. I made a mistake. I'll have to take the consequences. "But before you go, there's something I need to tell you."

Spring gives me a worried look. "I can wear makeup on my scar for the filming, if you want. I know how to cover it really well."

"Spring, no! Nothing like that. You look fine. It's just—"

At that moment Tree bolts into the store, almost crashing into a girl coming out. Spring rushes after him. As she hauls him back, he resists with all his might. "Sorry," she says to the girl. "He's harmless, really."

"No problem." The girl notices Spring's scar and grimaces. "He's so cute.

Love the boots." Tree is rocking a pair of well-worn Blundstones.

"Aren't they great?" Spring says. "Got them at the thrift store for a dollar."

"Cool." The girl clutches her Marlena's bag. "You know what? Please don't take this the wrong way, but you could totally use some makeup."

"Excuse me?" Spring holds Tree close to her.

"No offense or anything. But you're really pretty. And that scar is kind of not."

"Seriously?" Spring flicks her head so her hair falls away from her face and her scar shows more. "You have a problem with my scar?"

The girl looks horrified. "Omigod, no, sorry, so sorry. I was just trying to be helpful." She spins around and scurries away.

"Hey, why didn't you sign her up?" Lug wants to know.

"Forget it," I tell him. "Sorry about that," I say to Spring.

"Why?" she asks. "It's not your fault some people have no respect for boundaries."

"I know, but that was really rude and insensitive."

"I'm used to it." Spring ruffles Tree's hair. "We've had enough of the mall, haven't we?"

"Go home," Tree says. "Right now."

Spring checks her phone. "Dad's coming soon," she tells him.

"He is?" I hope I don't sound too panicked. But I still haven't told her I'm not Bo Blaketon. And now I've lost my nerve. I don't want to upset her after how mean that girl was.

"In about twenty minutes," she says. "Bo, do you ever wish you could go back and change something you've done?"

"Huh?" Does she know the truth? Has she figured it out on her own? Is she giving me a chance to come clean? Because realistically, how could she possibly believe I'm a TV star? "Well, um," I say, "yeah, of course." Totally. Like today. "Probably everybody does."

"I guess," she says. "If I could have a do-over, I wouldn't be so greedy. See, I wanted that stupid marshmallow so bad. My parents don't let us have much candy, and I couldn't let it fall in the fire." Her voice quivers as she speaks. "I wish I'd let that marshmallow burn. Instead of me. And then I wouldn't have this hideous scar."

I can't help myself. I've never hugged a girl in a romantic way before, but I slide my arm around her. "Hey, don't say that. You're so beautiful."

"Thanks, you're very sweet," she says. "And I know I'm beautiful inside. I go to a support group for kids who are disfigured in some way, and I've worked through all that. I know I'm more than my scar. I know I'm a better, stronger person for how I've suffered." She pauses and digs around in her purse to find some toys for Tree. "But I still wish it had never happened, you know? I'd like to be normal again."

"I get that." I pull her closer. I want to tell her that's what my mom says too. But if I start talking about Mom, I might start to cry or something. That wouldn't be cool.

"Hey, you guys," Lug calls, "I could use some help over here." But he's doing fine on his own. The girls going in and out of Marlena's gawk at me and Spring, then sign up.

"Later," I tell him. I've only got a few more minutes with Spring.

"So what about you?" she says.

"What about me?"

"What do you regret?"

This would be the time for honesty. But what comes out is, "I regret that you're leaving so soon."

"But we'll see each other next week, right, Bo? When we're on set?"

Can I make something up? Like how I'm not on camera at the same time as the extras? But acting like I'm really Bo Blaketon will keep the lie going. And that will only make things worse when she learns the truth.

Tell her, tell her, tell her, my brain says. But my voice says, "Yeah. Next week. Of course."

Chapter Twelve

We sit down on the bench together. I keep my arm around Spring. My fingers stroke her amazing hair. She doesn't object.

"So anyway," she says, snuggling close. "You wanted to tell me something?"

"I did?" *Tell her, tell her, tell her.* But all I want to do is kiss her.

"Before that nasty girl with the makeup advice came along," she says. "You were about to say something important."

"Oh, that." I need to handle this right. I take my arm from her shoulder to help Tree play with his toy cars. We push them up and down on the bench. That buys me some time to think. But no good way of admitting what I've done comes to me.

"Yes, that," she says. "What did you want to tell me, Bo?"

"Um, well, see, what I wanted to say was—oh, look, there's Dakota."

"Dakota?' Spring glances around.

"Yeah." I have a sinking feeling. This is not good. "Dakota is Laurence's older sister." I shouldn't have drawn attention to her. But I wanted to distract Spring.

Dakota is with a guy who is probably her boyfriend. Or one of them. They're outside the phone store next to Marlena's.

I hold my breath. Maybe she won't see us. Maybe she won't see Lug in front of Marlena's.

But she does.

The guy goes ahead into the phone store. Dakota calls to Lug, "Hey, loser! What's up?" She saunters over to where we are.

Lug follows her, acting all casual. "Nothing," he says. "Just hanging out." He's a master at staying cool. He doesn't look or sound guilty.

I'm starting to sweat. I'm tempted to run. But I don't want to leave Spring.

Dakota stands there with her hands on her hips, staring at me. "Thought you said you didn't have a girlfriend?"

There's nothing I can do to save this situation.

But I have to try. "Hey, Dakota," I say. "This is my new friend, Spring." I sling my arm around her shoulder again. "Oh, and her little brother, Tree."

"Really." Dakota raises her eyebrows. "You work fast."

Spring says brightly, "Have you signed up yet?" I can feel Spring admiring how good Dakota looks. I want to warn her that Dakota's not nice. That this isn't going to end well. But I can't find the words. I'm too scared.

Dakota squints at Spring's scar. "Signed up for what?"

"To be an extra on *Shatterproof*. They're filming in North Van next weekend. Laurence and Bo are signing up extras." Spring stops when she sees the surprised look on Dakota's face. "But I guess you already knew all that?"

"Sure, but not the details," Dakota says. "I don't work in the industry, and Laurence never tells me anything. He wouldn't want his big sister to be part of the show."

So Spring fills her in.

I sit there shuddering while she gushes on and on. This can't be happening.

Dakota listens like she believes every word. "Omigod," she says when Spring's done. "That's incredible!"

"I know, right?" Spring says. "It's such a great chance to be on TV and also make some money."

Dakota takes her time breaking the news. First she checks her phone again. Then she straightens her shirt and pushes the sleeves back. And then she says, all sweet and innocent, "Yeah, but see, there's only one problem."

Spring looks puzzled. "There is?" She picks up a toy car Tree dropped and hands it back to him. "What's that?"

"What's that?" Tree repeats. But nobody laughs.

Dakota points one of her long black nails at Lug. "Laurence over there is not a production assistant." Then she stabs me in the chest with her talon. "And this guy? He's not Bo Blaketon."

"Yes, he is." Spring doesn't get it yet. She turns to face me and says, "You are, right?"

I don't answer. The words won't come out. And I can't look her in the eye.

"Bo?" she says. "You did tell me that's who you are."

"Uh, no," I mumble. "I never actually told you that." I point at Lug like Dakota did, minus the long ugly fingernail. "He did."

Lug just stands there smirking. Like he can't wait to see how this plays out.

"Are you kidding?" Spring says. "Please tell me you're kidding."

"I wish I was," I say.

"Sorry. But no," Dakota says. "He's cute and all, but he's definitely not Bo Blaketon."

"Then who is he?" Spring sounds like she's going to cry.

Dakota delivers her punch line. "He's just my dorky little brother's dorky friend Nate."

"Is that true?" Spring asks me.

"Yeah, it's true."

Spring moves away from me. She stands, gathers Tree's toys and takes his hand.

"Sorry to burst your bubble," Dakota says to her. "But you shouldn't believe everything guys tell you." She leans in and studies Spring's scar. "Oh, and one other tip? With a face like that, wear makeup."

There's a beat of silence while her words sink in. I've no idea what to do or say.

Then Dakota says to Lug, "Wait till our parents find out what you've been playing at."

"Aw, come on, Dak," he whines. "You don't have to tell them." His earlier confidence is gone. Now he just sounds worried.

"But why wouldn't I?" she says. "Every time you mess up, it takes their focus off me."

Lug groans. "Okay, how about we cut you in? We've made almost four hundred bucks today. You can have fifty if you keep quiet."

"You've got to be joking," Dakota says. "Me get involved in one of your sick, creepy schemes? Didn't you learn anything from your grad-party photo thing?"

Then she shrieks with laughter and heads for the phone store. "You guys are so busted!"

Chapter Thirteen

After Dakota leaves, Lug says, "What a bitch. I hate her."

"No duh. She's a piece of work," I say.

Spring just stands there in shock.

I don't know what to do except start apologizing. "Spring, I'm so, so, so sorry."

She stares at me like I've murdered somebody. "That's what you wanted to tell me?" she says. "That you're not really Bo Blaketon?"

"Um, yeah, it is." Why oh why didn't I do it sooner? Like, before Dakota showed up? "I'm really sorry. I should have told you myself."

"Too bad you didn't," she says. "Too bad I had to hear it from her." She tugs on Tree's arm. "Come on, we're leaving."

"No, please don't go!" I follow them toward the mall entrance.

"My dad will be here by now," she says. "Thank heavens I called him to come early."

I trail after her, begging, "Please, wait a minute. I can explain."

"No, you can't," she says. "You lied to me!"

"Not on purpose."

"What?" She stops short and whips around. "How else do people lie?"

"I mean, it's not like that. I didn't mean to. I didn't want to."

"But you did. You sat there in the food court and let Laurence tell me you were Bo Blaketon. True or false?"

"True, but I had a good reason."

"Oh, please!" Spring turns and tugs on Tree's arm.

I can't let her get away. I hurry after them again. "It's true I did pose as Bo Blaketon this morning," I say, catching up. "But it wasn't planned. It was totally random. These girls thought I was him and it just kind of morphed from there. I never felt right about it, and I really wanted to quit, but Lug took incriminating videos of me. He said he'd tell my mom what I did and then he said he'd post them online if I didn't keep helping him. And my mom doesn't even know I'm here today. She thinks I'm at a cross-country meet in Victoria."

Spring won't look at me. "So you had to lie to me because you'd already lied to your mother? That's supposed to make me feel better?"

"Um, yeah, I guess," I say. "I mean, I hope so."

"Well, it doesn't. That's so twisted!" She breaks into a run to get away. Tree howls as she drags him along.

I chase after them. A couple of people turn to watch. I hope nobody calls security.

Tree stumbles, and Spring is forced to stop again. "Please," I say. "You have to listen. Lug was blackmailing me. That's why I did it."

Now she faces me. With a scowl. "Who's Lug?"

"Laurence. Lug's his nickname."

"Suits him. What a creep. You're both creeps!"

"No, he is. I'm not. But anyway, I couldn't let my mom find out because she's had a really hard time lately. She had a bad accident and she's in a wheelchair and she lost her job and then my dad left and I wasn't supposed to be hanging out with Lug at all, because of, um, that other thing Dakota mentioned."

Tree's shrieks fade to sobs. Spring kneels down to comfort him and wipe his nose. When she straightens up, she says, "And what exactly did Dakota mean about that other thing?"

"That wasn't my fault. Lug was responsible. He took photos of girls and Photoshopped them so it looked like they were doing bad stuff." She gives me a look. Like she's waiting for the whole story.

"Okay, I was there and I didn't stop him from taking the photos. But I didn't know he was planning to blackmail those girls. And he's not my friend anymore."

"Why should I believe you?" Spring starts walking again.

We're almost at the mall entrance. "Because I really like you. I want to see you again. And I just hope you'll give me another chance. *Please*."

Spring doesn't answer that. Instead she says, "I can't believe you said I could interview you! As Bo Blaketon!"

I try to defend myself. "I said maybe!"

"Same difference! You're a con man!"

"Not usually. Mostly I'm just Nate."

"Well, just Nate, you're sick!" she says. "I thought you were a nice guy! I trusted you!"

"I am a nice guy. You can trust me!" I grab her by the shoulders. "Please let me explain why I did it."

"Back off!" Without letting go of Tree, she pushes me away. "You let me help you get money from those girls! You made me a criminal too!"

I grab hold of her again. "Spring, please. Give me another chance."

"No way!" Her voice rises in anger. "Get lost, jerk!" She shoves me harder this time.

A security guard is on us in seconds. "Is he bothering you, miss?"

I step away from her, hands at my sides. "No, sir, I'm not. It was just a misunderstanding, but it's all good now."

Spring glares at me as she tells the guy, "That's right. He's not bothering me anymore. Ever!"

"Are you sure?" The guard isn't giving up easily. But, of course, that's his job. "Did he hurt you in any way?"

"No, really, he didn't. It's all fine." Spring peers out the entrance doors. "My dad's here to pick us up." She and Tree go hand in hand to the waiting car. They climb in, and it drives away.

"Okay, son, move along," the guard says.

"Yes, sir." I turn to go find Lug. He'll either be at the game store or RadRide. "I'm just leaving."

"Not that way, you're not." The guard grabs me by the shoulder.

"This way." He escorts me out of the mall. "And don't come back," he says. "I see you here again today, I call the cops."

I stride out into the parking lot so it looks like I'm really leaving. But I have to get back in there. I have to find Lug and get his iPad.

It's risky, but I don't have a choice.

Lug could still post those videos.

Chapter Fourteen

I circle the mall in a panic. I don't have any time to waste. My bus to the ferry is in half an hour. But I can't go back inside right away in case security is watching for me.

I dodge shoppers and cars, trying to think things through. How can I get Lug to delete those videos? How can

I make things right with Spring? How can I not miss my ferry?

I can't wait any longer. I go back in by another entrance and text Lug. **where r u?**

RR, he replies.

I rush to RadRide. He's at the checkout, paying for a ton of clothes.

"Whoa!" I say. "What is all this?"

"What's it look like?"

I see he's got those Vans and a hoodie I wanted. "Like you're buying half the store."

The cashier takes Lug's money. "Thanks for shopping at RadRide." She puts everything into bags. We both stare at her arms, inked wrist to shoulder with flowery vines. "Hey," she says to me. "You look familiar. I'm sure I've seen you on TV. Are you, um, oh, you know, what's his name?"

"No, I'm definitely not." I rush past Lug and out of the store.

"Hey, we could sign her up," he says, following fast. "I bet she'd want to be an extra."

"Are you crazy? Dakota's going to tell your parents!"

"Yeah, well, she might. Or she might just hold it over me." Lug heads for the food court. "But she probably will. That's why I spent all the money. If I wear everything right away, my parents won't be able to make me return it." He sits down at a table and puts on the Vans. "There's a start." He pitches his old sneakers into the garbage.

I can't believe this guy. "So where's my money from this afternoon?" I don't know how to convince Spring to give me another chance. But I figure doing something good with the cash will help.

"Sorry, Bo. Spent it all." Lug snaps the tags off the hoodie before pulling it on.

"What? That's not fair!"

"Seriously? What's not fair is that you spent all your time with Freakface. I signed up six girls while you were hitting on her."

"I wasn't hitting on her. And those girls wouldn't have signed up if they didn't think I was Bo Blaketon."

Lug removes the packaging from some Shoe Goo and grip tape. "Yeah, you were."

Okay, I was. But I'm not admitting that to him. "No, I was impersonating a TV star so you wouldn't rat me out to my mom or post those videos online."

Lug grins like he might still do both. "Sucks to be you."

Why did I ever think Lug was my friend? But now's not the time to get into it with him. "Okay, so you got what you wanted," I say. "With my help, you made more money this afternoon. So now I want you to delete those videos."

Lug gets his iPad out of his backpack. He sets it on the table and brings up the screen. "These are so great," he says. "You really do look like Bo Blaketon."

"But I'm not him," I say. "Delete those. Please."

Lug takes three new T-shirts from his RadRide bag. He cleans the gunk off the table with them. "Oops, those got dirty. Can't return them now."

"And besides the videos," I say, "you should delete the personal contact info for all the girls."

"Except Freakface? I'm sure you want her number. Oh, unless she already wrote it on your hand?"

I glare at him. "Not funny."

"You said it! Nothing funny about Freakface. She's just, you know, a friggin' freak!"

No point arguing with him. He's jerking me around. And I realize he's not planning to delete anything.

I'll have to do it myself. I almost reach for his iPad. But I don't want to clue him in. I'll have to get it when he's not looking.

I check the time on my phone. I've got ten minutes to catch my bus. The stop is across from the mall, but the street is crazy busy. It's almost impossible to cross without waiting for the Walk sign.

There's only one thing to do. Make him let down his guard. Beat him at his own game. "Actually," I say, "now that I think of it, you're right. Spring is really weird looking. I'd rather call one of those other girls. So you should keep all their contact info."

"Now you're talking," Lug says.

"And don't delete those videos either. We could maybe sell them to the girls. I bet they'd pay for a video of themselves with Bo Blaketon."

"Wow! You're way ahead of me, Bo! That's genius!"

"Yeah, but I have to catch my bus," I say. "I'm getting a drink to go. Want anything?"

"Sure, but let me get it. I owe you that much."

"Okay, thanks." We both stand to head for the snack bar. I let Lug go ahead of me. As soon as he's distracted, I grab his iPad.

Then I run.

It's a few seconds before he gets that I'm not right behind him. "Hey," he shouts. "Stop that guy!" He charges after me. "He stole my iPad!"

Folks turn to look, but nobody does anything. Just like when Spring was chasing Tree. "It's mine," I yell. "He stole it from me."

I race to the nearest exit, hoping security doesn't notice. Hoping nobody's got their phone out recording this. That's all I need.

Lug's still coming after me, but luckily he's not as fast. Thank goodness I've been training for cross-country.

I speed out of the mall and through the parking lot. When I reach the road I see a bus coming to the stop. I take a chance and dart across the traffic. Horns blare and brakes squeal.

But I make it.

Lug's still on the other side as I board. He looks majorly pissed off. I wave, and he gives me the finger.

I find a seat at the back of the bus and get to work.

Luckily, Lug's iPad isn't locked. The videos of me are still open. I delete them.

I send Spring's contact info to my phone. Then I delete everything about the girls we signed up. Everything Lug could ever use against me.

I breathe a huge sigh of relief. I'm saved. Everything's going to be fine.

The bus stops at the next corner. And the next. And the next.

That's when I realize this isn't the express bus.

Chapter Fifteen

I didn't stop to check the bus number. I just jumped on fast to get away. And now there's a good chance I won't make the five o'clock ferry.

My phone vibrates with a text from Lug. **Bring it back dickhead!**

I reply, **Check TransLink L & F**

Then I block his number. I used to know this guy, but I don't anymore.

And I don't think we'll ever be friends again. Not after today.

I take his iPad up to the driver. When we're stopped at a light, I tell her, "I found this back there."

She does a double take. "And you're turning it in?"

"Somebody's going to be looking for it. Can you make sure it gets to lost and found?"

She nods and tucks the iPad under her seat.

"You go all the way to the ferry along Seaview Drive?" I ask.

"Yup, it's the scenic route. Takes forever!"

"Great. Will we get there by five?"

"Not likely," she says. "But you never know."

People take their time boarding at every stop. Some load bikes onto the front of the bus. Some struggle with small children and huge strollers, some with shopping carts or luggage.

As the minutes tick by, my hopes fade. No way will we get there in time.

Unless the ferry is late. Which it often is. I check on my phone. But, wouldn't you know it, for once it's on time.

I make my way to the back doors. When we finally reach the terminal, I'm first off the bus. I race to the ticket window. It's still open, but sales stop ten minutes before sailing. No exceptions.

And just as I get there, the Closed sign flashes.

No! No, please, no!

Next sailing isn't until seven o'clock. So now I won't make it home before ten.

I'll have to think of something to tell Mom.

I slump on the steps outside the terminal and text her. **Will b really late. Sorry. Traffic on hwy. U ok?**

She texts back right away, like she's been waiting to hear from me. **Fine. Finished another scarf & started a sweater! How was meet? Did u have a good run?**

I don't want to lie to her anymore, so I just reply, **Personal best!**

She'll think I'm talking about my race. But what I really mean is, I finally stood up to Lug. And I met a girl I really like.

It makes me feel even more guilty when she replies, **Yr the best!!!**

I have to confess to her. I just don't know how.

I've got two hours to kill, and I'm starving. There's a fish-and-chips place near the terminal, but I spent most of my food money on the ice-cream sundaes. And no way am I using the money I got from the scam. So I just sit in the park and watch the five o'clock ferry sail away without me.

When the ticket window opens again, I pay my fare and go sit in the waiting room. I try playing games on my phone, but I can't concentrate. I keep thinking about Spring.

How can I make her forgive me?

And then there's the Dakota problem. She might keep our scam to herself so she can threaten Lug whenever she wants. But I have to assume she'll tell their parents.

And when she does, Lug will try to pin it on me. Just like he did with the grad photos. He'll say it was all my idea. And then his parents will call Mom.

It's bad enough that I lied about where I was today. She'll go ballistic when she finds out I pretended to be Bo Blaketon to get money from girls.

I have to tell her before she hears it from them.

I'd phone her, but this needs to be face-to-face.

I send Mom another text. **Have to tell u something. Talk when home.**

There. Now I can't change my mind.

I'll get there just as her evening CHW leaves. Mom will be in bed, but she'll still be awake. I hate to keep her up, but I have to tell her tonight.

She'll be heartbroken. But eventually she'll understand. Especially when I admit she was right about Lug. He's not a good influence. But, more important, he's not a good friend.

Once I've decided to tell Mom, I feel better. So much better that I have the nerve to call Spring.

But she won't talk to me. "Please don't call me anymore," she says and hangs up.

I call back right away, but I just get her voice mail. After three more tries I leave a long, rambling message. "Hey, it's Nate, and I just wanted to say again that I'm so sorry about today. But I want you to know that I've deleted all the contact info from all those girls, and if you give me your address I'll send you all the money I made and you can donate it to charity or whatever. And I'm not friends with Lug anymore, and I'm going to tell my mom the truth as soon as I get home. And I'm really, really sorry for everything, and I really, really want to see you again. Oh, and please, please, please, call me back."

I can only hope she'll listen before she deletes it.

It's time for the ferry, and I've almost given up hope when my phone rings. "Okay," she says. "Here's the deal. Do what you said with the money, and then we'll talk."

"Thanks so much for calling back," I say. "I appreciate you giving me another chance."

She makes a sputtering sound. "Don't blow it."

"I won't."

"I want to make a big donation to UNICEF."

"You will." A loading announcement sounds in the waiting room. Other walk-on passengers swarm past me. "Seriously. I've learned my lesson."

"Good to know," she says. "Because my grandparents live on the Island, and I'll be coming over to visit them at Thanksgiving."

Whoa! "So can we get together?"

"Maybe."

"Just maybe?"

"Just maybe," she says. "Don't push it."

"Okay," I say. "Just maybe. I'll take that."

I join the crowd and board the ferry.

I find a seat near the walk-off exit. I'll need to run when we dock to make my bus.

The ship's whistle sounds, and the ferry sails.

I stare out the window into the rainy darkness.

It feels like forever since I came over this morning. All I wanted was to get away and have some fun. Who knew I'd do something stupid and just want to go home?

Who knew I'd stop being friends with Lug?

Who knew I'd meet a girl like Spring?

Acknowledgments

With thanks to my family and everyone at Orca.

Jocelyn Shipley's YA books include *How to Tend a Grave, Getting a Life* and *Seraphina's Circle,* and she is co-editor of *Cleavage: Breakaway Fiction for Real Girls. Shatterproof* is Jocelyn's first book with Orca Book Publishers. Jocelyn divides her time between Toronto, Ontario and Vancouver Island. For more information, visit www.jocelynshipley.com.